# Impostors!

"Yes," Cindy whispered back as if from far away. A portion of her knew that her friends—if they were her friends—were trying to hypnotize her. But she lacked the will to resist. She did manage to turn her head away from Sally. But she just ended up staring into Adam's eyes, which were now directly in front of hers. His eyes were more frightening than Sally's, if that was possible. They seemed to burn with hateful red flames. He leaned close as she struggled to close her eyes.

"You have no power to resist us," he said in a cruel voice. "You are under our control. You will go home now and act as if nothing has happened. But later tonight we will come for you and take you and your little brother away." He grinned and his mouth was full of many sharp teeth. "We will take you to the Dark Corner."

# CHRISTOPHER PIKE

# SPOOKSVILLE #7™

## THE DARK CORNER

A MINSTREL® BOOK

Published by POCKET BOOKS
New York   London   Toronto   Sydney   Tokyo   Singapore

This book is a work of fiction. Names, characters, places and incidents are products of the author's imagination or are used fictitiously. Any resemblance to actual events or locales or persons, living or dead, is entirely coincidental.

A MINSTREL PAPERBACK *Original*

 A Minstrel Book published by
POCKET BOOKS, a division of Simon & Schuster Inc.
1230 Avenue of the Americas, New York, NY 10020

Copyright © 1996 by Christopher Pike

ISBN: 0-671-55066-7

First Minstrel printing April 1996

10  9  8  7  6  5  4  3  2  1

A MINSTREL BOOK and colophon are registered trademarks of Simon & Schuster Inc.

Cover art by John Youssi

Printed in the U.S.A.

I t was Sally Wilcox who brought up how cool Bryce Poole was and started the argument that led to their taking another trip through the Secret Path. Of course she later swore she had nothing to do with what happened. It was typical. No one, especially Sally, ever wanted to be blamed for starting an adventure, at least not in the middle of the adventure—when it looked like they would all die.

The day started as so many did that summer in Springville, known as Spooksville to all the town kids. Adam Freeman, Cindy Makey, Sally Wilcox, and Watch were together for a breakfast of milk and doughnuts. While stuffing their faces at the local coffee shop, they tried to figure out what to do with the day.

"Only a few weeks and we'll be back in school," Sally said, brushing her brown bangs out of her eyes. "We have to make the most of every day."

"I'm kind of looking forward to starting school here," Cindy, who was new to town, said. "I like learning things."

"Summer vacation in Spooksville is more of a learning experience than anything we do in school," Sally muttered.

"What is school like here?" Adam, who was also new to town, asked. "Is it as weird as the rest of the town?"

"It's pretty normal," Watch said.

"Except for a few of the teachers," Sally added. "The ones that aren't human."

"How did I know you were going to say that?" Cindy asked.

"There are a couple of unusual teachers in the middle school," Watch admitted.

Sally nodded. "There's Mr. Castro. He teaches

history, basically. But sometimes he talks about the future."

"Don't say it," Cindy interrupted, flipping her long blond hair over a shoulder. "Mr. Castro's really from the future."

"Well, he's not from around here," Watch said.

"I think he was built at the North Pole," Sally said. "If my sources are accurate."

"I heard it was the South Pole," Watch said.

Adam and Cindy exchanged looks. "So he's a robot?" Adam asked.

"He's not a desktop computer," Sally said.

Watch spoke reluctantly. "He does seem to have several machinelike qualities. For example, he never eats lunch. He never drinks water. When he's tired, he lays out on the football field and soaks up the sun's rays. I guess that's how he recharges his batteries."

"He also has a hearing aid that looks more like a cosmic receiver," Sally said. "He never takes it off. I hear it's wired directly into his positronic brain." She added, "He sure doesn't have trouble hearing."

Cindy shook her head. "I don't believe any of this."

"Wait till you get him for history," Sally said.

"And he pops his eyes out in the middle of a lecture just to clean his contact lenses."

"You said a couple of teachers were weird," Adam said. "Who's the other one?"

"Mrs. Fry," Sally said. "She teaches biology. She's a snake."

"She has scaly skin?" Cindy asked.

"Yes," Sally said impatiently. "I told you, she's a snake. When have you ever seen a snake that didn't have scaly skin?"

"What Sally means is Mrs. Fry seems to be part snake," Watch said. "She slides around the room and hisses all the time. Some people think she's a descendant of a reptilian race that lived here millions of years ago."

"Frogs are dissected all the time in her class," Sally said. "But never snakes or lizard. And all the frog parts—well, they disappear between classes. She eats them all."

Cindy made a face. "That's gross."

"You haven't seen gross until you've seen Mrs. Fry shed her skin," Sally said.

Adam didn't know what to make of any of this. "It sounds like it's going to be an interesting school year."

Sally brightened. "There are some cute guys at school."

Cindy was cautious. "Are they human?"

Sally waved her hand. "There's this one guy, his name's Bryce Poole, and he's so cool. He's like a young James Bond. Nothing disturbs him. You'll adore him, Cindy. He's got real dark hair, and super warm brown eyes. He's only twelve but he doesn't act like a kid. He talks like a well-read, sophisticated adult—like me."

Cindy was interested. "How come we haven't seen him this summer?"

"He's a loner," Sally said in a confidential tone. "He takes his own risks and he doesn't go whining to anyone about the consequences."

"It's hard to imagine anyone who's taken more risks than we did this summer," Adam muttered.

"And I can't remember that we ever whined to anyone," Watch added.

Sally stopped and laughed. "Are you guys jealous of Bryce?"

Adam shrugged. "How can I be jealous of someone I've never met?"

"I've met him and he's no big deal," Watch said.

"What bothers you guys more?" Sally persisted.

"Is it his obvious intelligence? His smoldering good looks? Or is it his dynamic attitude?"

"I told you," Adam said, "I've never met the guy. I know nothing about him."

"I'm trying to tell you about him," Sally said. "And you're getting all upset." She paused. "I think you're jealous, but you don't have to be. I like him as a friend. There's nothing between us."

"I bet he's wonderful," Cindy gushed.

"How can you say that?" Adam, who was a little insecure about his looks and especially about his height, demanded. "You haven't met him either."

"But if Cindy does fall in love with him when she meets him," Sally said, "you mustn't stand in her way, Adam. You have to be mature about it. So Bryce is better-looking, taller, and smarter than you and Watch. It doesn't mean you're not worthy human beings."

"Oh brother," Adam muttered.

"Where's a good place to meet him?" Cindy asked.

Sally spoke seriously. "You have to catch him coming or going. He never stays in one place long. He's always taking some super risk to protect this town from danger."

"Hold on a second," Adam said. "Since I've been

here, what has he done to protect this town? I mean, where was he when we had to deal with aliens, the Haunted Cave, the Cold People, not to mention the witch. Where was he all this time?"

"Yeah," Watch agreed. "Bryce didn't even bother to help us out with the Howling Ghost."

Sally smiled condescendingly. "Bryce doesn't deal with small crises. He only handles major ones."

"How can you call the Cold People a small crisis?" Adam demanded. "If we hadn't stopped them, they would have taken over the whole planet."

"Yes, but this isn't that big a planet," Sally said. "Not compared to the rest of the galaxy. Bryce deals more with cosmic emergencies."

"I thought you said he protected the town," Adam interrupted.

"And many other places," Sally said.

Adam and Watch looked at each other and rolled their eyes. "Like what kind of cosmic emergencies?" Adam tried again. "What is this big shot Bryce doing right now to protect us?"

Sally glanced around the coffee shop to make sure no one was listening. She spoke in a hushed tone. "Bryce is working with the Secret Path. He's trying to halt the interdimensional flow of negativity so that it doesn't seep into our reality."

Adam frowned. "How do you know this?"

Sally sat back and nodded gravely. "I have my sources."

"I don't believe it," Watch said. "Bryce Poole doesn't even know what the Secret Path is. I asked him about it once and he didn't even know where it began."

"He was just acting like he didn't know," Sally said. "After I told him about our adventures on the other side of it, he told me he didn't think you were equipped enough to survive the dangers of the interdimensional portal."

It was Watch's turn to frown. "Equipped with what?"

"I don't want to get personal here," Sally said.

"You are always personal," Adam said dryly.

Sally was offended. "Don't take it out on me because Cindy is suddenly interested in another guy."

"I didn't say I was interested," Cindy said.

"Your voice said it all," Sally corrected. "And I understand what Adam's going through. I'm sympathetic. To experience raging jealously and bitter rejection for the first time is not easy."

Adam sighed. "I am so grateful for your sympathy."

"We're arguing about nothing," Watch said. "Bryce isn't a super hero. He's probably not ever used the Secret Path."

"How do you know?" Sally shot back. "You've been afraid to use it since that first time."

"I haven't been afraid," Watch said. "I've just been busy with other things."

"Yeah, like saving the planet with me, his best friend," Adam added.

"I saved the planet, too," Sally said.

"Then you and Bryce should be perfect together," Adam said.

Sally laughed. "You are so jealous!"

Adam got angry. "Why should I be jealous of a guy who thinks he's James Bond? I agree with Watch. This guy has not been on the Secret Path. He doesn't have the guts."

Sally stood. "Why don't we go see?"

"Go where?" Cindy asked. "See what? What is the Secret Path?"

"It winds through town and leads to other dimensions," Watch explained.

"It starts or ends in the cemetery," Sally added. "Depending on how you look at it. Why don't we go there and look for signs of Bryce? Then we can see who the real hero in this town is."

"Why would Bryce leave signs that he's been using the Secret Path?" Watch asked.

"Yeah," Adam said. "Who is he trying to impress?"

"You guys have an answer for everything." Sally snickered and turned for the door. "Are you chickens coming or not?"

The way she worded the question, it was impossible to say no.

**2**

At the cemetery they had no trouble finding Madeline Templeton's tombstone. It was larger than all the other stones, and it had a large black raven carved on the top. The bird glared down at them and Adam was reminded of the last time they had taken the path, and the horror they had experienced. He shuddered as he glanced around the cemetery. The place was dismal. The few naked trees stood like angry skeletons. A shadow seemed to hang across the dry grounds, although there wasn't a cloud in the sky.

"Did you put this here?" Watch asked Sally as he knelt by Madeline Templeton's tombstone. He held up a green knapsack. Sally took a step forward and shook her head.

"No," she said. "Why would I put anything here? It probably belongs to Bryce."

"How convenient," Adam said.

Sally ignored him. "What is inside it?" she asked.

Watch opened the sack. "Binoculars. A thermos of water. A compass. A few flares." He held up a hunting knife. "It looks as if Bryce was anticipating trouble."

"But why would he leave his equipment here?" Cindy asked.

"I don't know," Watch said.

"I don't understand something," Cindy said. "How do you get onto this Secret Path? You guys said something about walking backward into the tombstone?"

"It's not that easy," Adam explained. "First you have to trace a route all over Spooksville. Then you have to walk from the front gate of the cemetery backward into the tombstone."

"Can't you just walk backward into the tombstone?" Cindy asked. "And forget the other stuff?"

"No," Watch said. "I tried it once and it didn't work. First you have to visit the location of each of the significant events in Madeline Templeton's life. You have to go to each place in order. Somehow that opens the portal to other dimensions."

"Then Bryce must have done that?" Cindy asked.

"I'm not convinced this stuff belongs to Bryce," Adam interrupted. "It doesn't have his name on it."

"You simply refuse to accept the fact that he is on the Secret Path," Sally said.

"What are we arguing about here?" Watch said, before another argument could break out. "It's possible Bryce is on the Secret Path—I admit that much now. But so what? What does it have to do with us?"

"Nothing," Sally said simply. "I was merely trying to make the point that Bryce is braver than you guys."

"Oh brother," Adam muttered.

"Well, you haven't gone back on the path," Sally said. "But he has, many times."

"The Secret Path is dangerous," Adam said. "If he's dumb enough to keep using it, that's his problem."

"It's only dangerous if you're not strong enough to handle it," Sally said.

"I can't believe you said that," Adam said. "You were the one who was against taking it in the first place."

"Wait a second," Watch said. "Sally does have a point. Remember what Bum told us when he spoke about the path. He said, 'The Secret Path doesn't always lead to the same place. It all depends on you. If you're a little scared, you end up in a place that's a little scary. If you're terrified, the path is like a road to terror.'"

"I'm sure Bryce is able to control his fear," Sally said. "And go where he wishes."

"Good for him," Adam said sarcastically.

"I'm not saying you have to follow him," Sally said.

"No, we definitely don't have to do that," Watch agreed.

"I mean, you don't have to try to impress me," Sally said. "I like you guys the way you are. I don't care how brave you are. Do you care, Cindy?"

"No," Cindy replied. But then she considered. "But I would like to meet this Bryce."

"He's a real hero," Sally said.

Adam and Watch both looked pretty disgusted.

"Do you think Sally's trying to push us onto the path again?" Adam asked.

"It feels like it," Watch said.

"Why, do you think?" Adam asked, ignoring the girls for a moment.

"I personally think that she's worried Bryce is trapped on the other side of the Secret Path," Watch said. "I think she wants us to rescue him, but she's too proud to ask for our help outright."

"My thoughts exactly," Adam said.

Sally didn't protest. They had hit a nerve. For a moment she stared straight ahead at the wicked tombstone, then finally she lowered her head.

"He's been gone a while," she said finally.

"How do you know?" Cindy asked.

"He told me he was going," Sally said quietly. "That was a week ago. I haven't seen him since."

"Is this his knapsack?" Watch asked. "Why did he leave it on this side?"

Sally shrugged. "I think it's his. I don't know why he didn't take it with him."

"Why was he using the path?" Adam asked.

"I told you the truth about that," Sally said. "He wanted to stop the overflow of evil into our dimension."

"At least he sets his sights high," Adam remarked.

"If we're going to take the Secret Path, we have to start now," Watch said, checking one of the four watches that he always wore. "It takes half the day to visit all the important places in Madeline Templeton's life."

"Wait a second," Adam said. "Before we go to all that trouble we have to decide if we *can* even help Bryce. There's no reason to think that we'll end up in the same dimension as he did. We might end up back where we were last time, and that's one place I don't want to be again."

"But if he is trapped," Sally asked, "how can you just leave him to an eternity of torment and agony?"

"Better him than us," Watch said wisely.

Adam put his hand on Sally's shoulder. "You're really worried about him, aren't you? That was just a show at the coffee shop, wasn't it? You've been trying to bully us into taking the path."

Sally nodded. "He's never been gone this long before. I'll go with you guys if you go." She paused. "I'm not afraid."

"Yeah, you are," Watch said. "We're all afraid to go on the path again, and we can't just talk ourselves out of our fear. And that means if we do take it, we'll end up in a scary place."

Sally nodded as she stared up at the tombstone. "In an evil place, the place where Bryce went."

The sequence they had taken before to get onto the Secret Path had been this:

1. The beach (where Madeline was supposedly born)
2. The Derby Tree (where Madeline cursed the tree and turned its leaves red)
3. A cave (where Madeline killed a lion with her hands)
4. The chapel (where Madeline got married)
5. The reservoir (where Madeline drowned her husband)

6. The beach (where Madeline was almost burned to death)
7. The cemetery (where Madeline was buried)

Obviously, going to the beach twice seemed stupid, but the sequence, they knew, was the key to success. Going to the cave and then to the chapel and then back to the reservoir was also inconvenient, since the cave was not far from the reservoir. But they knew they had to stick to what they had done before because it had worked.

It was close to four o'clock by the time they got back to the cemetery. Starting at the front gate, they walked backward through the cemetery to the tombstone, holding hands the whole way.

"Why do we have to do this?" Cindy asked, sounding nervous.

"Because Madeline Templeton was carried here upside down," Adam said. "This is our symbolic way of reenacting that event." He paused. "You sound scared."

"I am scared," Cindy said quickly. "I've never gone through an interdimensional portal before."

"We're really going to end up in a horrible place," Sally muttered.

"Maybe you shouldn't go with us," Adam said to Cindy. "You could stand guard on this side."

"What am I guarding?" Cindy asked, although she sounded interested.

"You never know what might come back through the portal," Sally said.

"It might be a good idea if one of us does stay on this side," Watch said. "If we don't return, the guard could go for help." He added, "I don't mind standing guard."

Sally glanced over her shoulder at the approaching tombstone. "I bet none of us would mind staying at this point." But then she suddenly let go of Cindy's hand. "But it should be Cindy. The rest of us are experienced with this portal."

"Are you guys sure?" Cindy asked, dropping Adam's hand and watching them as they continued to trudge backward toward the tombstone.

"You're the logical person to stay behind," Adam said, trying to reassure her. "There's no use going through the portal if you don't want to do it."

"Like we're all having a barrel of fun here," Sally remarked.

Cindy walked beside them as they stumbled backward. "I feel like a coward."

"You should," Sally said. "But I'll try not to tease

you about it." She paused. "If Bryce should reappear before we do, send him back to look for us."

"Have him bring his knife," Watch said.

"No," Adam said. "Cindy, grab the knapsack. I want to bring his stuff with us."

Cindy hurried to the tombstone and grabbed the bag. She handed it to Adam.

"How long should I wait here before I go for help?" she asked.

"If we're not back by dark," Watch said, "find Bum, tell him what's happened. He might be able to help."

"If he can be bothered," Sally added.

"We're just about there," Adam said anxiously. "Let's hold on to each other tight. Goodbye, Cindy. Wish us luck."

"Good luck!" Cindy called.

"I feel a whole lot better now that she's blessed us," Sally said.

They stumbled as they stepped onto the actual grave. Suddenly everything went black and he felt as if he were sinking. His friends seemed miles away. He couldn't see them. He was in the eye of a hurricane, where everything was perfectly calm, although he knew madness raged all around him.

**W**hen everything returned to normal, Adam realized they were in a place that was far from normal. It was Spooksville and it was not. As they looked around in wonder, they realized they were in a heavenly version of their home. A sweet scent filled the air. The surrounding trees were a lush green. Everything seemed to be glowing with a faint golden light, radiating love and joy.

"This isn't so bad," Sally remarked.

"It looks like paradise," Watch said, removing his glasses to clean them. "It's amazing we ended up in such a wonderful place, considering how scared we were."

"I wasn't scared," Sally said quickly, letting go of their hands. "I think it was me who lifted our overall vibes."

"I liked the way your arms shook so much when you weren't scared," Adam said.

"They only shook because I was holding on to your arms," Sally said, stepping away from the tombstone. She sucked in a deep breath of the sweet air. "I love this place! Look at the sky. It looks like one huge rainbow. I don't know if I want to go home."

Watch was concerned. "We tried the Secret Path to find Bryce. But if he's off fighting evil, I doubt that he's here."

"That's true," Adam agreed. Then he stopped and stared down at some initials carved into the base of the tombstone—**BP.** He pointed them out to the others. "Bryce Poole. He must have been here."

Sally bent over the initials. "It's only a couple of letters, but he could have carved them." She raised her head and stared out of the cemetery, which actually looked more like a park. "I wonder where he could have gone?"

"Let's walk into town and ask for him," Watch said, replacing his glasses. "I think I see people in the distance."

"Wait a second," Adam said. "We should figure out where we are before we talk to anyone."

"That's easy," Sally said. "We're in heaven."

"You mean we're in *a* heaven," Adam said. "This place is beautiful but it's still Spooksville. See, the castle's over there, and the ocean is down that way."

"What I mean is we don't have to worry about getting killed here," Sally said. "I think if Bryce is around, people will be happy to lead us to him."

"Then why did he carve his initials on the base of the tombstone?" Adam said. "He could have just set out a sign announcing that he was here."

"He might have been afraid of something," Watch agreed.

Sally laughed. "Nonsense! This is one place where I'm not afraid. Let's go explore. I think that Bryce is here, and when we find him he'll probably be having the time of his life."

"I hope you're right," Adam said.

They walked along the road that wound down

toward the ocean and the center of town. Along the way they passed the castle. To their immense surprise they saw Ms. Ann Templeton—or this dimension's version of her—supervising a picnic for a bunch of dwarfs and elves. She waved, and they didn't know what else to do so they waved back. They were having a barbecue of chicken and fish. Each of the dwarfs had a can of Coke, but the elves were all drinking orange soda out of clear glass bottles.

"See," Sally said. "Here she doesn't have nasty goblins working for her."

"I kind of liked Belfart," Watch mused. "I hope the marines accepted him."

"Maybe we should stop and talk to Ann Templeton," Adam said, thinking out loud. "Get the scoop on this place."

"No," Sally said. "I want to get into town. Bryce is probably there." She added, "I wouldn't mind going to my house to see what the Sally on this side is like."

"I don't know if that's a good idea," Adam said, although the same thought had occurred to him. "It might complicate things if we met ourselves."

"It might give us a mild case of schizophrenia," Watch agreed.

"You guys are no fun today," Sally said. "I'm dying to meet the heavenly version of myself—no pun intended. I bet I'm simply extraordinary."

"Well, there is a lot of room for improvement," Adam muttered.

Sally snorted. "I heard that. Come on, let's at least get something to eat. I bet the food here is delicious."

They ended up stopping at a fast food joint on the edge of town. In their normal Spooksville the place was called **FRED'S FAT FOOD.** But here it was called **FRIEND'S FANTASTIC FOOD.** Plus the guy at the counter didn't look anything like Fred, who had tattoos, dirty fingernails, and an apron stained with human blood. The handsome young man who took their orders had long golden curls and eyes as clear blue as the sky. In fact, he didn't even want to be paid. He pushed their money back when they set it on the counter. The food was on the house.

"I could get into living here," Sally said.

"Maybe that's why Bryce didn't return," Watch said. "He liked it so much he just decided to stay."

"Whatever he decided doesn't matter; we have to go back," Adam said. "Cindy's waiting for us. She'll be worried."

"If she hadn't been such a coward she could be with us here now," Sally said.

"You thought she should stay," Adam protested.

"And I'm glad she did," Sally said. "She was so scared—we probably all would have ended up in some dark corner of the universe."

Their food arrived and it was wonderful. Really, it tasted better than any meal they'd ever had in their lives, and it was just hot dogs and french fries. Sally was so pleased by the food that she ordered a vanilla milkshake, which she refused to share with Adam.

"You can still get fat in heaven," she said. "I wouldn't want that for you if we're going to live forever now."

When they were about to leave the place, Adam struck up a conversation with the young man who served them. He listened patiently while Adam explained how they were searching for a friend named Bryce Poole. Adam asked Sally to describe Bryce. When they were through, the man spoke in a sympathetic tone.

"You three aren't from around here, are you?"

"Not exactly," Adam replied. "We're sort of from a neighboring city."

The man nodded. "I understand. We get people like you now and then."

"You do?" Sally asked, amazed.

"Yes," the young man said. "And the best thing you can do is go find your counterpart in the city. Once you find him or her, everything will be all right."

"That was exactly what I wanted to do," Sally said, looking rather pleased with herself.

Watch was confused. "So you know we're not from this dimension?"

The young man with the golden hair smiled. "That's obvious to all of us."

"You mean everyone in the city knows we're strangers here?" Adam asked.

The man ignored the question. "Find your counterpart and everything will become clear." He paused and stared off in the distance. As he did a strange light shone in his eyes. "I think they're waiting for you at Adam's house."

"Waiting for us?" Watch asked. "How do they know we're here?"

The man just smiled again. "You better hurry. You don't want to keep them waiting."

Feeling confused, Adam left the restaurant with his friends. Sally insisted that they head straight for Adam's house. But both Watch and Adam were having doubts.

"He didn't really answer our questions," Watch complained.

"He said our other selves would help us," Sally replied. "He was a nice man—we can trust him."

"He *seemed* like a nice man," Adam said. "But I agree with Watch. His answers were too vague."

"I don't care what you guys say," Sally replied. "I'm going to see my better half. I can hardly wait to have a deep and meaningful conversation with her."

"This will be one argument she's finally going to lose," Watch said.

Since they didn't know why they were reluctant to go, Adam and Watch agreed to accompany Sally to visit their other selves. Finding Adam's house wasn't difficult because it was exactly where it was in the other Spooksville.

Their three counterparts were sitting outside Adam's house.

They smiled when they saw Adam and Cindy and Watch.

All six of them smiled.

Then the counterparts stood up and slowly walked toward them.

As they did so, their faces began to change.

They began to melt. Into hideous demon forms.

# 5

It was too late. The three demons—they even had horns now—were on them in an instant. Adam was struck across the face with a scaly hand—his arms yanked behind his back. He felt a sharp pain in his spine, and he dropped Bryce Poole's knapsack. For a moment everything went black, and Adam thought he would pass out. Then he realized he was being dragged toward a steel pole, which he had not noticed a second earlier. It stood in the center of his yard, spiked chains hanging off it.

The yard was no longer the same. All around him

the scenery was changing, becoming darker and dirtier, lit with a chilling red glow. The heavenly version of Spooksville was turning into a hellish realm. The demon that had hold of Adam leered in his face. The creature's teeth were sharp, his eyes like those of a wicked cat, green and splintered with thick red veins. The nails on his claws were sharp like razors. He hissed at Adam.

"We have you now, fool!" the demon said as he snapped Adam's wrists into cuffs attached to the chains. Beside him, Adam saw the same torture happening to Watch and Sally. They both had demons leering in their faces. Adam's demon giggled, "You're never going to escape!"

Adam fought to remain calm. "Who are you? What is this place?" The town continued to change into a nightmare realm of ruined buildings and howling creatures. Up and down the street Adam could see many poles where people had been chained. Most hung lifeless, little more than skeletons, but a few still struggled to break free. The demon tugged at Adam's hair and slobbered on his shirt.

"Who am I?" the demon asked. "I am you. I am your dark half. And this place is the Dark Corner.

Those who come here from your world never return."

"But everything was so nice at first," Adam said.

The demon howled. "We always put on a show for newcomers! You humans are so stupid!"

Adam tried to sound brave even though he was terrified. Most of the other prisoners looked as if they had been there for ages.

"What are you going to do with us?" he demanded.

"Let you rot until the Gatekeepers come to judge you," the demon said. He yanked hard on Adam's head, pulling out a clump of hair. He held it up for Adam and the others to see. "With this I can enter your world, and become you! My partners and I will pass through the Secret Path and ruin everything that is yours!"

"No!" Adam pleaded. "Wait! Can't we talk about this?"

But the demons weren't listening. Along with his partners—who had also torn out clumps of hair from Watch's and Sally's heads—he put the hair in his mouth and slowly chewed it down. Then, by some wicked miracle, he began to change back into the form he had assumed when they had first seen him. Now he looked like Adam, and the other two demons once again resembled Watch and Sally.

"Now we have a piece of you inside us!" Adam's demon sneered. "We're free to go where we wish!"

"You can't go into our world!" Sally shouted at the demons. "You'll never get away with it! Our friends will spot you immediately, and you'll be destroyed."

Adam's demon laughed in her face. "By the time your friends know who we are they'll be here with you! Rotting in the Dark Corner!"

"But maybe we can work out a compromise," Watch suggested. "I can see why you don't like living here. It's a nasty place. We have ghettos back in our world that are like this. Maybe we can help you find a better place to live, and you can let us go."

The demons howled with delight. "We don't want to let you go!" Adam's demon said. "We love it when humans suffer! We live for suffering! Come, my pals, let's go play with these fools' friends!"

The demons danced away, heading in the direction of the cemetery and the interdimensional portal. Adam had never felt so miserable as he did right then. His wrists weren't simply chained, they were pinned above his head, and the spikes in the wrist cuffs were digging into his skin. Watch and Sally looked equally uncomfortable. All around them the air was filled with fumes and ash, making it difficult to breathe. Adam coughed as his throat dried out. Sally hung her head as if she were weeping.

"I'm sorry," she said. "It just seemed like such a nice place."

"The demons made it seem that way so that we would drop our guard," Adam said grimly. "But don't blame yourself. We were fooled as well."

"But we probably wouldn't be in this situation if it wasn't for you," Watch added truthfully.

"That's true," Adam had to admit.

Sally moaned. "I said I'm sorry. What else am I supposed to do?"

"If you could reach Bryce's knapsack, we might get his knife and try to pick these locks," Watch suggested. The backpack was closest to Sally. "See if you can catch the strap with your foot."

"I'll try," Sally said and strained forward with her right foot for the bag. Just another two inches and she'd be able to reach it, but even arching her back and kicking out, the tip of her shoe just missed the straps. After a couple of minutes of struggling she gave up and sighed. "I can't do it. What are we going to do now?"

"Probably rot for eternity," Watch said.

"Don't say that," Adam said. "We have to maintain a positive attitude."

"I don't know if a positive attitude helps when you're in hell," Sally mumbled.

"We're not in hell," Adam said. "We're in *a* hell. That's not exactly the same thing."

Sally stared down the street at the other captured people. A few were moaning and a couple even had bird nests on top of their heads. Black ravens screeched in their dry hair. Sally sighed again.

"Right now I don't think it makes much difference," she said.

"Look," Adam said, trying to sound upbeat, "we've been in difficult situations before and we've always managed to find a way out. We'll do the same this time. We just have to come up with a plan."

"We're waiting," Watch said.

"Well," Adam said. "First we have to break out of these chains. Let's concentrate on that."

"I don't think the power of our concentration is going to break these chains," Sally said.

"I can't believe you guys are ready to give up," Adam complained.

Watch nodded down the block. "It looks like a tall demon is coming. I hope it's not one of those Gatekeepers the others mentioned. They didn't sound all that friendly."

Watch was right. Another monster was approaching.

Cindy was lying in the grass beside Madeline Templeton's tombstone when the others reappeared. Because she was resting with her eyes closed, she heard them before she saw them. She was surprised because they had only been gone a few minutes. She sat up when she heard them talking and watched them as they stood huddled together in front of the tombstone.

"You guys just left." She was so relieved to see them again she broke into a huge grin. "Did you find Bryce?"

They paused and stared at one another as if

surprised by her question. Then Adam said in a flat voice, "We weren't looking for Bryce."

Cindy got up slowly. "But that's why you went on the Secret Path. Don't you remember, Sally?"

Sally broke into a smile at being addressed. She was looking around as if she had never seen the cemetery before. "We didn't find him," she said in a rather heavy voice. "But it doesn't matter. We don't need him."

Cindy was confused. "But you were worried about him."

"He's gone," Watch said simply. "He's not a problem. Take us to town."

"What did you see on the other side of the tombstone?" Cindy asked. "Anything exciting?"

For a moment their eyes brightened. Indeed, it was as if a faint red light shone in them. Cindy blinked her own eyes, thinking she must have imagined the glow.

"Would you like us to show you what we saw?" Sally asked.

Cindy shrugged. "Yeah. If it's safe."

Adam turned to Sally. "We're not showing her anything right now. We have things to do here first. Later we will take her."

"Where will you take me?" Cindy asked.

Adam smiled strangely. "To a nice place. We will take you there tonight."

"I don't know if I can go out tonight," Cindy said. "I think my mother wants me to stay in to watch my little brother."

"We'll take him with us as well," Sally said, stepping forward. "Enough talk. We want to go to town. We have much to do."

"OK," Cindy said, puzzled by their rude attitudes. "We can go to town. Where do you want to go?"

"We need food," Watch said. "We need meat."

"Do you want to go to Harry's Hamburgers?" Cindy asked.

"Yeah, let's go get Harry!" Adam squealed.

"Let's go eat Harry!" Sally yelled.

"Eat his meat!" Watch joined in.

Cindy forced a smile. "You guys must be real hungry."

At Harry's, Cindy's friends continued behaving oddly. They ordered two hamburgers each, nothing else, not even drinks. Then they stopped Harry before he began to cook the food.

"We like our meat rare," Adam said.

"We like it raw," Sally added, as she grabbed one

of the uncooked hamburgers and stuffed it in her mouth. In four huge bites she had devoured the whole thing. Cindy stared in amazement. Sally didn't chew at all. She was eating as if she were an animal. Cindy sat down at one of the tables and shook her head.

"What happened to you guys on the other side of the Secret Path?" she asked.

They all grinned. "We had fun," Adam said. "That's all. Don't you believe us?"

"No, I don't," Cindy said. "Something happened to you over there. Tell me what it was."

"What if we don't want to tell you?" Sally asked in a deadly tone.

"I don't know," Cindy said nervously. "I'll do something. I'll talk to Bum."

Watch came and sat beside Cindy. He put a hand on her shoulder. When he spoke a big bite of uncooked hamburger showed in his mouth.

"You had better not talk about us," he said. "We get mad when people do that. We get very mad and then we do *things.*"

Cindy stared at him as if struck. "What do you mean? What kind of *things?*"

Watch leaned closer. "Horrible things," he said softly.

Cindy's mouth quivered. "Watch," she said. "What's wrong with you. You never talk this way."

"He's talking just fine," Sally said as she sat on the other side of Cindy. She put a hand on Cindy's bare leg, and Cindy felt as if she were being touched by a lizard. Sally was staring at her with strangely bloodshot eyes. Cindy wanted to look away but found she couldn't. For a moment it seemed that only Sally's eyes existed, eyes that didn't really belong to her friend at all. The pupils of Sally's eyes were windows that opened onto a place of fire and pain. They bore into Cindy's brain, and Sally leaned over and whispered in her ear. Cindy noticed then how cold her breath was, and how it stank of something Cindy could not identify.

Out the corner of her eye Cindy watched Adam approach Harry, who had come around the counter. He was curious about what they were up to. Harry didn't make it all the way around the counter. There was a swift movement and then Harry sat down. Or maybe he fell over, Cindy could not be sure. Suddenly she was unsure of most things. She heard Sally speak in her brain more than in her ear.

"We are normal," Sally whispered. "We are the way we have always been. You are not to talk to anyone about us. If you do talk about us, you will feel pain. We will make you feel pain."

"Yes," Cindy whispered back as if from far away. A portion of her knew that her friends—if they were her friends—were trying to hypnotize her. But she lacked the will to resist. She did manage to turn her head away from Sally. But she just ended up staring into Adam's eyes, which were now directly in front of hers. His eyes were more frightening than Sally's, if that was possible. They seemed to burn with hateful red flames. He leaned close as she struggled to close her eyes.

"You have no power to resist us," he said in a cruel voice. "You are under our control. You will go home now and act as if nothing has happened. But later tonight we will come for you and take you and your little brother away." He grinned and his mouth was full of many sharp teeth. "We will take you to the Dark Corner."

**T**he demon that approached was taller than the others and thinner. He was also dressed differently. He wore a gray cloak instead of a furry hide, and he walked more like a man than a demon. The earlier demons had danced and jumped around like hungry animals, but this demon headed straight for them as if he had important business to complete. Adam had no doubt that he was one of the dreaded Gatekeepers, and that after he had judged them, he would torture them to his heart's content.

The three friends looked anxiously at one another as the demon neared.

"Maybe we can reason with him," Sally said.

"Like we reasoned with the others?" Watch asked.

"Whatever happens," Sally said, "I don't want to go first. And don't tell him it was my idea we came to this horrible place."

"Go first with what?" Adam asked.

"With whatever he's going to do to us," Sally said.

"Don't worry," Watch said. "He'll probably lower us into the boiling pit together."

"Shh," Adam said. "He's almost here. Don't give him any ideas."

The demon arrived a minute later. He stood directly in front of them and silently studied them. His face was as ugly as the other demons', with scaly skin, a wide slobbering mouth, and piercing green eyes. As he scanned the street, it seemed as if he was whispering to himself.

The whispers sounded vaguely human.

"What are you three doing here?" he asked, keeping his head down.

"It wasn't my idea to come," Sally said quickly.

"We mean you no harm," Adam said. "We came here looking for a friend."

"What is this friend's name?" the demon asked.

Adam squirmed against his pole. "His name is not important," he said. "At least not to you. He's our friend. We only want to find him and leave this place."

"Your counterparts have stolen some of your hair?" the demon asked.

"Yes," Watch said.

"Then it is not easy for you to leave here," the demon said. "They have probably crossed over to your world by now. You cannot return until they come back here." He paused. "Or until they are forced to return here."

Adam wondered at all the information the demon was volunteering. "Who are you? Are you a Gatekeeper?"

The demon spoke in a whisper. "I am not a Gatekeeper. But one will soon come for you. You must not let him take you. If he does, you are doomed. You will never escape here."

"You speak like a friend," Watch said. "Are you here to help us?"

The demon nodded. "I am here to help." As he spoke he reached up and peeled back his face, and they saw that he was wearing the mask of a demon. In the sober red light of the hellish realm a handsome young boy with dark hair and brown eyes stared at them.

"Bryce!" Sally exclaimed. "I knew we'd find you!"

Bryce put his finger to his lips and glanced once more up and down the streets. "Shh! Don't say my name so loudly. I am a hunted man."

"But you're only a kid like us," Watch said.

"Here I am a great danger to the Gatekeepers' power," Bryce said firmly. "I have been here almost a year, fighting their powers of darkness."

"But I saw you last week," Sally said.

"Time moves differently in the Dark Corner," Bryce said. "There is so much suffering here that time passes at a crawl."

"It's moving pretty slow for us right now, chained here," Watch said, trying to stretch his arms. "Can you loosen these cuffs?"

Bryce nodded and picked up his knapsack. "It's lucky you brought my supplies. I'll be able to pick your locks."

"Why did you leave your knapsack on the other side of the Secret Path?" Adam asked.

"I have left supplies at a dozen different portals along the Secret Path," Bryce said, taking the knife and working on Sally's cuffs. "I came here with another knapsack, but have since had to trade my supplies to get this disguise."

"Who traded with you?" Adam asked.

Bryce spoke in a hushed tone. "There are many creatures in the Dark Corner who hate the Gate-keepers. They are willing to help if you give them something in return. But they're all scared, even the best of them. They won't risk their lives to help me escape from here." Sally's cuffs popped open. "That's why I need your help."

"Was it true what you said?" Adam asked. "That we cannot return to our world until the other demons return here?"

Bryce was grim. "That is the rule. And none of your demons will willingly return. They will stay in Spooksville as long as they can."

"But then we're trapped here forever," Sally moaned.

"No," Bryce said. "I wasn't tricked like you were. Everyone told me to go see my counterpart, but I was suspicious. I hid out and tried to learn how things work here. I finally saw someone meet his counterpart and saw how the world changed after the illusion had served its purpose." Bryce nodded down the street. "That poor soul is chained over there. He has already been judged by the Gatekeepers and condemned to an eternity of rotting on a steel pole."

"Do the Gatekeepers ever let anyone go?" Watch asked.

"Rarely," Bryce said. "You have to be a saint to escape their judgment." He finished opening Watch's cuffs and turned to Adam. "My counterpart knows I'm here. He searches for me constantly. But as long as I don't touch him, I'm safe."

"But if he hasn't got you, can't you just leave here?" Adam asked.

Bryce shook his head. "It's not that simple. I need my counterpart to open the Secret Path for me. That's the way it is in the Dark Corner. There's no easy way out. But I can't drag my counterpart to the tomb. You saw how strong yours were. He would just overpower me, steal a lock of my hair, and escape to our world."

"What are they doing in our world?" Adam asked, anxious to be free of the cuffs. Already his arms were aching.

Bryce was obviously worried. "They cause pain wherever they go. It is their nature. Tell me, did you leave anyone guarding the other side of the tombstone?"

"Cindy Makey is waiting for us there," Sally said. "You know her, Bryce. She's that homely girl who moved here a few weeks ago."

"She's actually very nice-looking," Adam said.

Bryce nodded. "I know who she is. We must assume the worst, that the demons have already got to her." He unsnapped Adam's cuffs.

"Thanks," Adam said. "What will they do to her?"

"First they will try to control her mind," Bryce said. "Then they will bring her here to be judged by the Gatekeepers. They will try to bring as many as possible here. They will force them through the Secret Path. Because they're demons they don't have to hike all over the city to enter the Secret Path."

"What can we do?" Sally asked.

"You must help me catch my own counterpart," Bryce said. "Remember, I can't touch him. You must overpower him and drag him to the tombstone. If his hand touches the stone, that will be enough to open the portal for me. Once I'm on the other side, I'll deal with your demons."

"How do we know you won't just leave us here?" Watch asked.

"Watch!" Sally exclaimed. "How can you ask

such a thing. Bryce is a hero." She paused and added, "You really will come back for us, won't you, Bryce?"

"Yes. But I can't promise that I will be able to handle all of your demons. I will do the best I can." He glanced up at the sky. "Come, it's getting dark. If you think this place is bad now wait until then. All the demons run wild at night, and they're starving. They love nothing more than to eat a human alive."

"Sounds like a party," Sally muttered sarcastically.

# 8

Bryce knew where his own personal demon was. Seemed the monster was fond of hanging out at the beach. As they crept around the boulders of the jetty, they spotted him digging in the sand, searching for crabs. When he found one he would pop it in his mouth and swallow without chewing. He wouldn't even bother washing off the sand. He was an ugly little runt, but Bryce warned them once again how strong he was.

"We can't take him by force," Bryce said. "Even the three of you could not handle him in his normal demonic state. You would end up all bitten and bleeding and he would just get away."

"Do demons have a weak spot?" Watch asked.

"Yes," Bryce said. "They're sensitive to the cold. Notice how he doesn't actually let the water touch him, and this water is much warmer than the water at home. Cold slows them down. They're used to all the hellish fires here. What I'm going to do right now is fetch a glass of cold red lemonade. I know a place where I can get it. Then one of you is going to walk by and offer it to him. Tell him that it's a glass of human blood. A demon can't resist blood. He'll gulp it down before he realizes how cold it is. That should knock him out, or at least make him easier to handle."

"How come you haven't tried this before?" Watch asked suspiciously.

"You know the answer to that," Bryce said. "I can't get near him. He'll recognize me. But he won't recognize any of you, not if you wear my mask and robe."

"I'll give him the drink if the guys are too afraid," Sally said. "I trust you, Bryce. Did you know it was me who wanted to rescue you?"

"That's not what she wanted to tell the Gate-keeper," Adam muttered.

Bryce wasn't interested in their arguments. He warned them to keep his demon in sight and keep their heads down, then he disappeared. Watch and Adam were doubtful.

"I don't know if I trust this guy," Watch said.

"I know what you mean," Adam said. "But I don't know if we have much choice."

"What's wrong with you guys?" Sally demanded. "Bryce is the salt of the earth. He rescued us once already. You should be grateful."

"He rescued us so we could rescue him," Watch said. "Once he disappears through the Secret Path we have no guarantee he'll come back for us."

"He himself said he's been here a year," Adam told Sally. "That's a long time in this kind of place. It could have changed him somehow. He might not be the same Bryce you said goodbye to last week."

Sally was annoyed. "Bryce is strong, inside and out. If anyone could survive here, it's him. What are you saying anyway? That he's in with the Gatekeepers?"

"That's a possibility," Watch said. "The moment he's through the portal, they might attack us."

"Maybe he's worked out some kind of deal with them," Adam agreed.

"Nothing changed," Sally growled. "You guys are still jealous of him because he's so cool and competent."

"I'll believe he's competent if he manages to get our demons back through the portal," Watch said.

Adam sighed. "I hope they haven't been too rough on Cindy."

"I think the demons will be a good influence on her," Sally said. "Cindy needs a few rough edges to give her more personality."

Bryce returned ten minutes later. In his hand he had a dirty glass of ice-cold red lemonade. He held it out for Sally to take but she seemed doubtful.

"How can your demon be so stupid to think a glass of lemonade is a glass of blood?" she asked.

"Demons as a whole are pretty stupid," Bryce said. "That's the only reason I've been able to survive here as long as I have."

"But what if the demon only drinks a little of the lemonade?" Adam asked. "Just enough to make him mad? He could attack Sally and hurt her." He paused. "I should go in her place."

"I don't care which one of you goes," Bryce said. "I just need to knock this guy out as soon as possible. Remember you've got three demons running around Spooksville right now."

"Give me your costume," Adam said. "Let's get this over with."

Adam donned Bryce's demon suit and took the glass of cold lemonade. Trying to act like a normal demon out for an evening stroll, Adam walked in the direction of Bryce's demon. The monster looked up before Adam was halfway to him.

"Hi," Adam called. "Caught any good-tasting crabs?"

The demon snorted and slowly stood. He eyed Adam suspiciously. Adam wasn't as tall as Bryce. The disguise didn't fit as well as it should have.

"What do you want?" the demon demanded.

"A whole bunch of human kids came through the Secret Path today," Adam said. "You probably heard about them. We've been over with the Gatekeepers drinking their blood. I have a glass here if you want it. I'm stuffed—I don't think I could get another drop down."

The demon took a step closer and stared at the glass. "Is it fresh blood?"

"Sure. Just drained it out of a fat kid myself. Have a taste, you'll love it."

The demon was still suspicious. "What's your name?"

"Belfart," Adam said, remembering the name of the goblin in the witch's castle who wanted to join the marines. The demon snorted.

"That sounds like a goblin's name," he said. "Where are you from? I haven't seen you around here before."

Adam didn't believe he could stand a lengthy questioning. He decided to act more annoyed, more like a real demon.

"Listen," he said impatiently. "If you don't want this blood, it's fine with me." He raised the glass to his lips. "I'm not that full after all. I think I'll just finish it myself. Hmm—this is going to be good. Nothing like a glass of *warm* human juice in the evening."

The demon didn't like that. In one swift move, he grabbed the glass from Adam and threw the drink down in one gulp. Then the glass fell from the demon's hand, and he stared at Adam with the most peculiar expression, even for a demon.

"That must have been one cold kid," he mumbled.

Then the demon's eyes closed and he fainted on the spot.

"Hurry!" Adam called to the others, who were watching from behind the jetty.

It was almost dark by the time they were able to drag Bryce's demon to the cemetery. The demon weighed more than they would have thought for such a small guy. Watch, Adam, and Sally had to do all the work. Bryce continued to maintain it wasn't safe for him to touch his counterpart. He told them to lay the demon beside the tombstone, but not touching it.

"He will wake up as soon as we put his hand on the portal," Bryce said.

"You know an awful lot about demons," Watch remarked.

"You know how everything works here," Adam added.

"That's because I've kept my eyes and ears open since I got here," Bryce said sternly. "If you had done the same you wouldn't be in the mess you're in now. You wouldn't have rushed off to meet your counterparts."

"They sometimes make poor decisions," Sally said quietly.

"Night's coming," Adam said. "How are we supposed to survive here until you return with our demons?"

"You'll just have to do the best you can," Bryce said. "But whatever you do, stay near here. I can't say exactly when I'll been shoving your demons through, but you have to be right here. Otherwise you won't get back."

"What do we do when you shove them through?" Watch asked.

"The portal will open," Bryce said, "and you'll be able to jump through."

"Do you know where Cindy lives?" Adam asked.

"Yes," Bryce said. "I'll go straight to her house and see how she is. I promise." He nodded to his demon slumped on the ground. "Now press his palm against the tombstone. Like I said, it will probably wake him up. You must be prepared to fight him off."

"How do we do that?" Sally asked, suddenly not so sure about her super hero.

"Do the best you can. I'll return as soon as I can." Bryce paused and glanced around. "Place his hand on the tombstone. Do it now."

Adam did as Bryce said. Several things happened simultaneously. The tombstone glowed with a strange white light and Bryce leaped into it and disappeared, taking his knapsack with him. Then the demon shook his head and opened his eyes, looking angrily around.

"Hey," he said when he saw them. "You're the humans I heard about. You're the ones with the warm blood. Come here, I'm thirsty."

**9**

**W**hen the knock came on the door, Cindy almost screamed. Her mother had gone out for the evening, and her little brother had a cold and was already in bed. In a sense she was all alone in the house. Even though it wasn't completely dark, she was terrified to be alone. Ever since she had said goodbye to Adam, Watch, and Sally, she had been trembling. They had said that they were coming back for her, and even though they were her friends, she was terrified of seeing them again.

And she didn't know why.

She was so confused.

Her brain felt as if it were working underwater.

The person knocked at the front door again.

Cindy felt like crying. She wanted to remain silent and hope they went away. She tried that, in fact, but whoever was at the door was persistent. The knocking continued, growing harder and harder. Clutching a folded magazine for protection, foolishly, she crept to the door.

"Who is it?" she called softly through the door.

There was a pause. "This is Bryce Poole. Are you Cindy?"

She coughed. "What do you want?"

"I have to talk to you. It's important. Open the door."

"No. I don't know you. Go away. Come back tomorrow."

"I can't. This is an emergency. Your friends are in danger."

"My friends," Cindy muttered, not sure how she was supposed to complete the sentence. She didn't want to talk about her friends, she didn't want to see them. Yet they had told her they were coming back for her. Why did that thought fill her with dread? She saw them practically every day.

"Open the door," Bryce demanded.

"What do you want?" Cindy asked again. "My friends are not here."

Again Bryce paused. "I know," he said quietly, so softly she almost didn't hear him through the door. "They're trapped on the other side of the Secret Path."

Cindy choked. "That's impossible. I saw them."

"It wasn't them, Cindy. It was demons who had stolen their forms. Please open the door."

Cindy finally did as she was told. Bryce practically jumped inside, and then quickly closed the door behind him. Cindy was pleased to see he was as cute as Sally had said. Unfortunately she wasn't in the mood to enjoy his company. He stared at her anxiously.

"What?" she muttered.

"Look into my eyes," he ordered.

"Why?"

"Do it!"

Cindy stared into his eyes, and as she did so the memory of staring into other eyes, much darker eyes, came back to her. Sally, Watch, Adam—they had done something to her with their stares! Cruel red flames blazed in her head, even though she felt a terrible chill in the pit of her stomach. She turned away and buried her face in her hands, tears burning her eyes.

"What's happening to me?" she cried.

Bryce put a hand on her shoulder. "The demons used their power on you. They tried to bend your will to theirs. But it's all right now. The spell is broken."

She looked at him. "Who are you? How do you know about demons?"

"Sally told you about me. My name is Bryce Poole. For a long time I have been exploring the many sides of the Secret Path. There I discovered many wonderful things, and many horrible things. I have just come from the worst place of all—the Dark Corner. Your friends are trapped there now. They cannot return to this dimension until we capture their counterpart demons and force them back through the interdimensional portal."

Cindy put a hand up to her head. She couldn't keep up. "I don't understand. My friends returned through the Secret Path. I saw them. I went and ate with them."

Bryce shook his head. "Those were not human beings who returned. They were demons. You must have noticed how weird they acted. Even when a demon tries to hide it, his cruel nature comes out. And I know they used the power of their eyes on you. That's why you feel so confused. But the worst of it has passed. You're free to do what you wish. You can help me if you want, and I do need your help."

Cindy had to take a breath. "They were acting so strange. I do remember staring into their eyes and seeing fire. But then, everything after that is crazy." She paused. "This is like some kind of nightmare. I just feel like I have to wake up."

Bryce was grim. "There will be no relief until we get your friends back. Tell me, what time did the demons say they'd come back for you?"

Cindy strained to remember. "I don't know. They didn't give a time. But I got the impression it would be late at night. I know there were things they wanted to do first."

"What kind of things?"

"I don't know! If they're demons, like you say, could they hurt other people?"

A shadow crossed Bryce's face. "They can do much worse than hurt people. They can drag them back to the Dark Corner, to the Gatekeepers."

"Who are they?" Cindy gasped.

Bryce shook his head. "It's better not to talk about them, not when it's almost dark." He stepped to the window and peered out through the drawn curtains. For the first time Cindy noticed he was carrying a knapsack. "We must search for them, stop them before they capture any more people."

"Shouldn't we get help?" Cindy asked.

"No one will help us. No one will believe us. We have to do this ourselves, and we must do it now."

"But I can't leave. I'm watching my little brother. He's asleep upstairs."

"It's better if you leave here. It'll be safer for him. Remember, the demons want you in particular. Your brother will stay asleep. He won't know anything is wrong."

"But where will we look for them? They could be anywhere."

Bryce was thoughtful. "Each of these demons is the counterpart of one of your friends. Even though they are completely evil, they are connected to Adam, Watch, and Sally. There is a good chance that they'd do what your friends would do after returning through the Secret Path."

"You mean, go home?" Cindy asked, horrified.

Bryce nodded. "It's possible. At least it gives us a place to try to pick up their trail. Let's hurry to

Adam's house. It's closest, and Adam is the natural leader of the group. His demon is probably as well."

"What do we do when we catch up with them?"

Bryce allowed himself a faint smile. "I have studied these monsters for a long time. Don't worry, I have a few tricks up my sleeve."

**10**

Adam never doubted Bryce so much as when Bryce's demon woke up and tried to attack them. Adam felt as if Bryce had set up the whole thing. Of course Adam didn't have much of a chance to be angry at Bryce. Not with a demon climbing to his feet and demanding their blood. The demon eyed Adam up and down. Adam still had his demon costume on, except for the head, which sort of ruined the effect.

"Hey," the demon said. "You're the one who gave me that red-colored ice-cold lemonade. That gave me a terrible headache. You owe me. Give me your arm and open a vein."

"You think he would at least say please after making a request like that," Sally remarked.

"Grab some sticks!" Adam yelled, reaching for a branch himself. The trouble was, in this particular dimension, there weren't a lot of heavy branches lying around. Adam came up with a stick that probably wouldn't have frightened a goblin, never mind a demon. The others did about as well. Yet the demon seemed upset that they were arming themselves. He continued to rub his ugly head.

"I am not in the mood to fight," he said. "But if you wish to surrender, I will be happy to drink your blood and bring your cursed souls before the Gate-keepers."

"Somehow that doesn't appeal to us," Sally said.

The demon turned away. "Then I'm going for my partners. They'll be more than happy to fight with you and eat you alive. Stay here until we get back."

Adam shook his head as the demon left. "Bryce gave us the same instructions. And it looks like it's going to get us killed, or worse."

"You have to quit blaming Bryce for all our problems," Sally said.

"We could blame you," Watch said.

Adam sighed and threw down his flimsy stick. "I don't want to blame anyone. I just want to go home. We can't stay here, but if we leave we'll miss our chance to get back through the portal."

"That is *if* Bryce returns with our demons," Watch said. "For all we know he could be at home already, watching TV."

"Maybe a *Twilight Zone* rerun," Adam agreed. "To remember us by."

"I have faith in Bryce," Sally said. "If he can't save us, he'll die trying."

"That should be the least he'd do after leaving us here," Watch grumbled. He checked his watches. "They've stopped. This dimension's got heavy time distortion on top of everything else."

"We've got to come up with a plan of action," Adam said. "Sorehead, Bryce's demon, and his friends will be back soon." He paused. "The only thing I can think of is to run."

"Can demons run fast?" Sally asked.

"Like we're all experts on demons," Watch said.

Sally frowned. "You're in a bad mood."

"It must be because I'm about to be tortured to death," Watch said. He turned to Adam. "Where should we run?"

"I've been thinking about that," Adam said. "This place is gross and disgusting, but it mirrors our Spooksville as far as its design. I'm thinking it probably has a chapel in the same place our town has a chapel. We might be able to hide there for a while. I imagine demons would stay away from there."

"But we have to time our return to this spot to match Bryce's return with our demons," Watch said. "And that is next to impossible with the time differences and Sorehead and his friends chasing after us."

"We'll just have to hope for the best," Adam said, cocking his head to the side. "Do you guys hear that?"

Sally jumped. "Yeah. It sounds like a bunch of screaming demons, coming this way. That Sorehead sure moves fast."

Adam began to back up. "We better do the same. Let's head out the back way and circle around to the chapel. I just hope we can make it that far."

"I just hope the demons don't hold parties there," Sally muttered.

\* \* \*

They managed to make it to the chapel, but the going was rough. It was fully night now and the dark had brought about more evil changes in the town. In many places huge fissures had opened in the ground, out of which shone steaming red light. From these holes they thought they heard pitiful screams.

Yet the chapel looked much as it did in their Spooksville, perhaps a bit more neglected. The place definitely needed paint and a good cleaning, but the walls and windows were reasonably intact. In fact the chapel was one of the best-kept buildings in the entire Dark Corner, and Adam felt a measure of relief. He was sure the demons could not enter the building. Hurrying inside, he locked the door behind them and hoped they would be safe for the time being.

"Maybe we should go to church more often," Watch said, looking around.

"It's got to be a safer place to hang out than in the cemetery," Sally said, plopping down in one of the pews.

"But not as exciting," Adam said, trudging toward the altar.

"I could use a little less excitement in my life," Watch said.

Sally was astounded. "I can't believe you said that. Fearless Watch, who is always ready for the next big adventure."

Watch removed his glasses and cleaned them on his shirt. "I'm still disgusted that we will probably be tortured and eaten before dawn."

Adam spun around and looked back at his friends. "I hear the mob again! They're coming this way!"

It was true. The howls were growing louder by the second.

Sally jumped up. "We have to get out of here!"

Watch put his ear to the back door. "No. It's too late. They're already on the same street. We'd be cut down as soon as we stepped outside. We've just got to trust that they won't enter this holy building."

"Is any building holy in this evil dimension?" Sally asked.

The demons surrounded them a minute later. Adam and his friends could see them through the stained-glass windows, dozens of them. Their burning torches sending shafts of light across the wooden pews. Their hideous faces glaring at them with hunger. Yet in the midst of the attack Adam smiled.

"See," he said. "We're safe. They're afraid to come inside."

But a minute later the gang smelled smoke.

The demons were not afraid to set the chapel on fire.

**11**

Cindy and Bryce caught up with the demons outside Adam's house. Apparently Adam's family was out for the evening. The front door of the house lay wide open and the stereo blared onto the front lawn. The demons danced on the grass, kicking and spitting on each other as they did so. They had the radio tuned to a heavy metal station. Cindy peered at them from around the side of a neighboring house.

"They look like they're having fun," she said, having doubts about Bryce's story.

"They're just getting warmed up for a night of destruction and evil," Bryce said.

"Is it possible you're wrong?" Cindy asked. "Maybe they weren't changed on the other side."

"You forget," Bryce said. "I was with the real Adam, Watch, and Sally. These are definitely impostors." He nodded. "See how they spit and curse each other. Is that normal?"

"For Sally it's not completely unusual." Cindy paused and listened as the three characters giggled together. A chill went through her body and once again she saw the cold red flames in her mind. "Never mind," she said quickly. "I believe you. What do you want to do?"

"We have to get their attention and force them to follow us." Bryce dug in his knapsack. "We have to lead them to a place where they'll be vulnerable, but also a place they'll want to enter."

"Where's that?" Cindy asked.

Bryce pulled a couple of flares out of his bag. "A meat locker at the grocery store. Demons are always hungry for raw meat. When they see it, they lose all control. They run toward it and start eating. If we can get them to run into a meat locker, we'll be able to shut the door on them and they'll soon pass out. Demons can't stand the cold. In fact, they'll remain unconscious for a while. During that time we should be able to drag them up to the cemetery and open the Secret Path so that we can rescue your friends."

Cindy thought his plan was brilliant, except for a few small details. "How do we get them to follow us into a meat locker?"

Bryce gestured with the flares. "If we light one of these, they'll be drawn to the burning red light. It reminds them of the Dark Corner. They hate the evil realm, but it's the only place they really feel comfortable." He stopped and glanced around. "But demons are fast. We have to have bikes to keep ahead of them."

"Adam has a bike in his garage," Cindy said. "Wait! He has two of them. Watch left his bike in Adam's garage yesterday because he was going to work on it there. It's not like it's really broken or anything, so we can each have a bike. If we sneak around the side of Adam's house, we can go in the side entrance of the garage."

"Good," Bryce said. Then he stopped. "But maybe you should wait here. I can do this myself. There's no reason for you to risk your life."

Cindy smiled darkly. "My friends are in danger. That's the best reason I know of to risk my life.

Plus I can probably outpedal you. None of the other kids can keep up with me." She held out her hand. "Give me one of those flares."

"Maybe I do need you," Bryce admitted as he reluctantly handed over one of the flares. "You realize that to get them into the meat locker at the grocery store one of us has to run into the locker ahead of them. Whoever it is, the other one will have to close the door."

Cindy swallowed. "With the person inside with the demons?"

"Yes. The demons might kill whoever's inside before the cold slows them down. Promise me, if I get there first, you'll shut me inside with them. You can't hesitate."

"Will you shut me inside with them?" Cindy asked.

Bryce spoke gravely. "I'll have no choice. It will be the only way to stop them."

Cindy nodded weakly. "I understand. Let's do it now, before I have too much time to think about it and get scared."

Sneaking around the side of Adam's house and into his garage wasn't difficult. With the noise of the blaring stereo, the demons couldn't have heard a battalion of marines approaching. But now came the tricky part. Bryce insisted they ride straight out the front of the garage, with at least one of the flares burning.

"We've got to pass close by them to make sure they see the burning red color," he said. "It's the only way to drive them wild, and make sure they follow us."

"What grocery store are we headed for?" Cindy asked.

"Fred's Foods. It's open twenty-four hours a day. Ann Templeton shops there every Friday evening."

"You know her? We were in her castle."

Bryce nodded. "I heard about that. You were lucky to get out alive." He glanced through the garage window at the demons. "We'll both be lucky to survive tonight. Get on that bike and get ready. I'm going to trip the garage door opener. Save your flare for now. Mine should be enough to grab their attention."

With that, Bryce struck his flare. In the dark of the closed garage, the burning color struck a knot of fear deep into Cindy's heart. How similar the light was in color to the light that had blazed in the three demons' eyes at Harry's Hamburgers. Briefly, Cindy prayed that Harry was all right. Vaguely she remembered Adam's striking him, and the man falling to the floor. Adam must be a demon to knock out a grown man.

Bryce pushed the garage door opener.

Cindy positioned herself on Adam's bike, ready to take off.

The garage door creaked upward.

The demons came into view.

They had stopped their dancing.

They were staring at Bryce and Cindy.

"Go!" Bryce cried as he shoved forward on Watch's bike.

The demons were as quick as Bryce had predicted. Even though Bryce and Cindy were on bikes and had the whole yard between them and the demons—and supposedly the element of surprise—the demons almost grabbed them as they swept by. In fact, one of the demons—it was Sally's—reached out with long nails and managed to scratch Cindy's left arm. Cindy felt a stinging sensation and then the trickle of blood over her skin. She cried out as she pedaled into the center of the street, pushing the bike harder than she had ever pushed anything in her life. Beside her, Bryce barely kept ahead of Adam's and Watch's demons. The flare burned in Bryce's right hand and the demons howled at the sight of it.

"Head for the center of town!" Bryce called over. "Stay ahead of me!"

"I'm trying!" Cindy called back.

"Remember what must be done!"

"I remember," Cindy replied, but quietly, more to herself. Straining to stay a few feet ahead of the demons, she felt more afraid than she could ever remember. And the worst part was still to come. How could she close the door on Bryce and leave him to the demons' mercy?

And what if he had to close the door on her?

Ten minutes later it looked like that might be what had to happen.

For some reason, after only ten minutes, Bryce's flare began to go out. It must have been defective. Cindy knew most flares were designed to burn for at least a half hour. Of course there was no time to take the thing back to the store and complain. For all she knew, Bryce had bought it at Fred's Fat Food. The bottom line was that she now had to strike her own flare. As she did so, the demons immediately focused on her. Fortunately, just before the grocery store there were two hundred yards of downhill riding, and she knew she'd be able to put a small distance between herself and her pursuers. Bryce called over to her. His flare was all but dead.

"Throw me the flare!" he said.

Cindy glanced over her shoulder. The demons' eyes burned as they had that afternoon. She had to fight not to stare into them, to be drawn into their evil depths. Inside, she could feel them willing her to slow down. She wasn't completely free of their spell.

"No!" she called back. "There's no way you can catch it! You'll burn your hand!"

"I don't mind a little burn! Throw me the flare!"

"No! They'll get away! I'll lead them where I have to!"

Bryce stared over at her for a moment before answering. "You can't do that, Cindy! This is my plan!"

"I'm a part of your plan!"

"No! You'll be killed!"

Cindy drew in a deep breath and pushed the bike forward as they hit the bottom of the downhill portion of the road. She replied to Bryce but not with a shout. It may have been she was simply talking to herself.

"I won't be killed," she said.

The wind flew in their faces. The flare blazed in her hand. The demons screeched at their backs. As the grocery store neared, Cindy decided she wouldn't perform a normal braking. Instead she would slide the bike into the front door of the store like a baseball runner sliding into home plate. The move, she hoped, would get her a couple of seconds' headstart for the meat locker.

But then what?

They would just chase her inside.

Bryce would just lock her inside.

The grocery store was fifty yards away now. Twenty.

Bryce began to brake.

Cindy began to tilt her bike on its side.

Her unusual strategy allowed her to stop on a dime. The only problem was that she went down with the bike, and dropped the flare in the process. She barely had time to grab it and climb to her feet before the demons ran onto the parking lot. Bryce was only a few feet behind her, his hand out-stretched.

"Give it to me now!" he shouted.

"No way," Cindy snapped. Turning, she dashed into the store.

The market was relatively empty, and it was fortunate that Cindy had been in the place before. She knew exactly where the meat section was, and therefore where the meat locker must be located.

Racing down the cereal-and-sugar aisle, she could hear the demons shrieking at her back. They sounded both mad and excited at the same time.

Cindy dashed into the rear of the store.

There was no clerk in sight. The meat locker was on her right. A steel door into a wasteland of red meat. Without looking over her shoulder, because she was scared about what she would find, Cindy grabbed the thick handle and pulled it down and open. Inside, it was dark as a cave, as cold as a bottomless well. Holding her burning flare up, Cindy strode forward. Thick slabs of beef hung all around her, like the forgotten victims of some insane war. She hurried to the rear of the freezer, and it was only then she dared look behind her.

The three demons stood in the doorway of the freezer.

They grinned and stepped forward.

"Hi," the one who resembled Adam said. "We told you to wait at home until we came for you."

"We told you we don't like to be disobeyed," the Sally demon said.

"We told you how we would eat you alive," the Watch demon said.

The three of them giggled and drew closer.

Behind them, through the open door, Cindy

caught a glimpse of Bryce. She almost shouted to him that she made a mistake. That she didn't want to be locked inside with these monsters. She almost cried out for mercy. But the shout died in her throat. Bryce stared at her with sad eyes, and then he slowly shook his head. His right hand was already on the thick metal door. He seemed to be closing it slowly, but maybe it was just Cindy's imagination. When the door was finally shut, and the dark settled over her heart as well as her eyes, and the demons' eyes began to glow a wicked red, Cindy prayed that this whole situation was only in her imagination. That she would wake from the nightmare soon.

But the demons just kept coming closer.

# 12

When the inside of the church was transformed into an inferno, Adam and his friends were forced to flee outside. They were all choking on the smoke and were immediately taken captive by the horde of demons. Bryce Poole's demon, Sorehead, supervised their capture. He seemed pleased with himself for recapturing them and had them bound at the ankles and wrists with steel cuffs. He said they were now going to be taken before the Gatekeepers and judged. Adam thought that would be better than being eaten alive, but after listening to Sorehead for a few minutes he wondered.

"You'll be brought before a judge," Sorehead explained as he led them through the horrible night of the Dark Corner. Demons surrounded them and kept trying to grab them. Adam and the others soon got tired of fending them off. Sorehead continued, "There will be a prosecutor and you will be defended by a lawyer. There is also a jury."

"Which of these is a Gatekeeper?" Adam asked.

"They're all Gatekeepers," Sorehead said. "They change jobs. It gives them a little variety. Next week your lawyer might be a judge."

"You mean, our lawyer is a demon?" Adam asked.

"Sure," Sorehead said.

"And the jury?" Sally asked.

"All demons," Sorehead said. "You're in the Dark Corner, after all. What do you expect?"

"But how can we be judged fairly if everyone's a demon?" Adam asked.

Sorehead chuckled. "What is this concern with fairness? We're demons. We're not supposed to be fair." He paused and rubbed his head. "Whose idea was it to give me that cold red lemonade?"

"It was your counterpart in our world, Bryce Poole," Watch said.

"Where is he now?" Sorehead demanded.

"He escaped through the portal," Adam said. "He used your palm to open it."

Sorehead appeared momentarily angry, but then he laughed. "He escaped and left you behind! You've got to hand it to him, he's got a lot of me in him."

"We wouldn't disagree with that," Watch said, throwing Sally a look. But Sally looked too miserable to defend Bryce anymore.

After a mile of walking they went into one of the huge red fissures that had opened in the ground. After traveling through a cinder-filled underground tunnel, they eventually came to a huge cavern. The space was surrounded by a volcanic pool. The glowing lava provided the chamber with its red glow, and also made it uncomfortably hot. The sweat that dripped off Adam's forehead was from fear as well as from the heat.

In the center of the chamber sat the judge, the prosecutor, and the twelve demon members of the jury. They were resting on seats carved of black volcanic stone. The judge's seat was the highest of all, and the judge himself was a big fat demon with brilliant red hair and purple eyes. He was larger than most human adults. He sneered at them as they entered, and Adam received the distinct impression that he wasn't on their side. On the table in front of him sat a large black book.

Close to these demons was a massive silver-colored balance scale. It was old-fashioned in design, basically just two metal plates with a weight in the center to balance the two plates. Beside the far plate stood a tall thin demon. He oversaw a huge bag of thick gold coins. Adam had no idea what the scale was for, but figured he would learn soon enough. Sorehead ushered them before the judge and jury. There he smacked them each on the head.

"Bow your heads to the judge and act respectful," Sorehead said. "Remember, you're in a court of law."

Just before they did bow, they each glanced over at their lawyer. He was short and chubby and had a big cigar hanging out of the side of his mouth. His eyes were blood red and his hair was like straw that had been dipped in crude oil. He was a real sleaze.

"Can't we hire our own lawyer?" Sally muttered as she lowered her head.

"You can't afford one," Sorehead replied. "You should be grateful one has been appointed for you by the court. This guy's name is Foulstew, and he's not bad."

"We should at least be given a human lawyer," Watch grumbled, his head also down.

Sorehead snorted. "He wouldn't try too hard to defend you."

"Why not?" Adam asked, his eyes focused on the floor in front of him.

"Because we would just eat him if he won," Sorehead explained. "We would tell him that ahead of time."

"Silence in my courtroom!" the judge boomed, clearing his throat. "The prisoners may approach the bench."

Sorehead kicked each of them in the butt and they trudged forward. They were forced to raise their heads to see the judge reading from a large piece of burnt paper.

"This trial concerns the case of the fine demons of the Dark Corner versus the wicked and ill-mannered humans of Spooksville, namely, Adam Freeman, Sara Wilcox, and Watch." The judge paused, raising a dirty eyebrow. "What happened to your last name, Watch?"

Watch shrugged. "I use it so seldom, I forget it."

The judge turned to the thin demon next to the scale. "A token against the accused, Scalekeeper!" he snapped.

The Scalekeeper took a gold token out of his bag and placed it on one plate of the scale. Immediately that side lowered. Watch spoke to Sorehead.

"What does that mean?" he asked.

Sorehead was amused. "It means you've just thrown away a valuable point. If I were you, I'd watch my mouth."

The judge pounded his gavel, which was a human skull. "Order in the court! The charges against the accused are as follows. Being human. Eating our hot dogs without paying. Escaping from the torture poles. Tricking one of our outstanding citizens with fake blood. And burning down our chapel." The judge set the paper aside. "How do you plead?"

"We didn't burn down the chapel," Sally said. "You burned down the chapel."

"But you disgusting humans forced us to burn it down," the prosecutor said, stepping forward. He was perhaps the strangest-looking demon of all. He was extremely short and compact. The top of his head was flat, in fact. It looked as if a huge weight had landed on him, and crunched him into a compact parcel. His eyes were particularly wicked—more like a lizard's than a cat's. Worst of all, he wore a cheap wrinkled three-piece brown suit. The prosecutor continued, "My name is

Bloodbutton and it is my job to see that each of you burns for your sins."

Their own chubby attorney with the bad-smelling cigar stepped forward. "And my name is Foulstew and I'm here to have a good time!" He laughed. "And maybe to get you off, if you deserve it, which I doubt."

"And I'm the judge here and all of you shut your mouths so we can get this trial going," the judge said. "How do you three plead? Innocent or guilty?"

Adam turned to Foulstew. "How should we plead?" he asked.

Foulstew rubbed his oiled hair and took a puff on his cigar. "If you plead guilty, you will be taken from here immediately and tortured for the rest of your lives."

"What if we plead innocent?" Sally asked.

"You will easily be proven guilty and tortured for the rest for your lives," Foulstew said. "I mean, at the very least, you're human, which is a serious crime in the Dark Corner. It alone carries a penalty of forty years of having your nails slowly pulled out of your hands while your toes are being tickled."

Adam frowned. "Isn't there a third way for us to plead?"

"Objection!" Bloodbutton shouted. "The defendant is trying to take unfair advantage of this court."

The judge pounded his skull. "Overruled! You may answer your clients' question, Foulstew, but please don't tell everything."

Foulstew bowed in the direction of the judge and then spoke to Adam and his friends. "It is possible for you to enter a plea of what we call Virtues versus Vices."

"What does that mean?" Adam asked.

Foulstew nodded to the scale. "We seat you on one end of that scale, and if you outweigh your vices—when we are through reviewing your life— then you get to go free. For each vice we find in you, the Scalekeeper will add one of those *heavy* gold coins onto the other side of the scale. Obviously, if there are too many gold coins, you will be outweighed and you will lose."

"But what about our virtues?" Adam asked. "For each one of those do you take a gold coin off the other side?"

Foulstew glanced at the judge. "I ask Your Honor's permission to respond?"

The judge frowned. "Counsel may respond. But

let this court warn counsel that the jury would like at least one of these humans for dinner tonight."

Foulstew glanced uneasily at the jury before answering Adam's question. "That is correct. For each virtue or noble deed you are able to demonstrate in this court, one gold coin is removed from the scale. In other words, if you are a good enough person, the charges against you will be dismissed and you will be allowed to go free."

Adam turned to Sally and Watch. "We have led pretty good lives, for the most part. We should be able to win this way."

"I wouldn't be too sure of that," Sally said. "Remember what Bryce said. You practically have to be a saint to avoid being condemned."

"Do we have a choice?" Watch asked. "I say we go this way."

"Me too," Adam said.

Sally shrugged. "I've been as good as you guys, maybe better. I'll go for it, too."

Adam turned to Foulstew. "We want to enter a plea of Virtues versus Vices."

Foulstew looked disappointed. "I would advise against it."

"Why?" Watch said. "You just said the other

ways we're sure to be found guilty and be tortured for the remainder of our lives."

"Yes," Foulstew said, glancing at the jury of twelve demons. "But you probably will be found guilty this way, too. Only this way you might get me in trouble. You wouldn't want to do that, would you?"

"We don't care if you get in trouble," Sally snapped.

"What she means is we won't say anything that implicates you in our crimes," Adam said quickly, not wishing to lose the good will of their defense.

"What crimes are those?" Watch grumbled.

"Your first crime is that of being human!" the judge interrupted. "Watch! Climb onto the side of the scale closest to you and sit down without moving. And keep your mouth shut."

Watch did as he was told. Naturally, since there was only one gold coin on the other side, the scale immediately sunk down on Watch's side. That was good. If he could stay heavier than the other side, he would go free. But then the Scalekeeper raised his bag of gold coins and poured on so many that Watch bobbed up in the air. Adam and Sally were outraged.

"You can't do that!" Adam shouted. "You haven't proven he has any vices!"

"I just said he was human!" the judge shouted back. "That is an immediate vice, and the penalty is one's weight in gold. Add to that the coin Watch received for insulting me, and you can see why the scale is tipped against him."

Adam turned to Foulstew. "You didn't tell us that we would have our whole weight against us before we started."

Foulstew spread his hands. "You didn't ask, Adam. Honestly, I am doing my best to defend you, and I am one of the best lawyers in all of the Dark Corner."

"How many humans have you successfully defended?" Sally asked.

"None," Foulstew admitted. "But I keep getting closer with each case."

The judge pounded his skull on his table. "Order in the court! It is time to weigh Watch's virtues and vices. Bloodbutton, Foulstew—prepare to present your evidence! And may the powers of darkness guide your words!"

Sally sighed and leaned over to whisper in Adam's ear. "We're never going to get out of here."

**13**

At first, as the demons closed in on her, Cindy just froze. Her terror was that great. She could see no way out of her situation. She was locked in a dark freezer with three hungry monsters. She knew she was already dinner. And they would probably eat her alive.

But then she remembered the reason they tricked the demons into the freezer. Bryce had said the cold would knock them out. Perhaps if she could stop them for a few minutes, she might give the cold a chance to do its job. They were so intent on getting her, she realized that they had not noticed that the door had been closed behind them. Cindy thrust her burning flare out in front of her.

"Stop!" she ordered. "Or I will burn you!"

The demons giggled. Already their faces were changing, becoming less human. Adam's demon had sprouted horns and Watch's had fangs. Worst of all was Sally's demon, which had snakes writhing on top of its head instead of hair. For some reason, though, the snakes did not look totally out of place on Sally's head. It was Sally's demon that first responded to her threat.

"We don't care if you burn us," she said. "We're used to burning. Where we come from, we burn every night."

"Yeah," Watch's demon said. He held out his arm, and Cindy saw that it had begun to grow scales. "Go ahead, burn my arm. Burn me a fresh tattoo. Have it say that I love human meat."

"Raw human meat," Adam's demon added as he reached out with clawed hands. "Kicking and screaming as it goes down our throats."

"Wait!" Cindy shouted. She gestured to the sides of hanging beef. "What about all this hamburger here? You guys had hamburgers this afternoon. You liked those pretty well. Or why don't you have some prime rib? I'll even cut you a few slices, and maybe cook you up some potatoes and onions."

The demons looked disgusted. "We'll eat hamburger during the day if we must," Sally's demon said. "But at night we like something a little more juicy." She moved a step closer. "Like you, for example, you little troublemaker. I think I'll eat your eyes first, and make you watch me."

Watch's demon scowled at Sally's demon. "If you eat her eyes first, how can she watch? She'll be blind."

"Then I'll eat her ears first!" Sally's demon yelled.

"I get the ears!" Adam's demon shouted. "They're my favorite bit, next to the tongue. I'll eat that first and listen to her scream!"

"If you eat her tongue," Watch's demon pointed out, "she won't be able to scream. She won't be able to talk at all, even to tell us how much she is suffering. We should eat her tongue last."

"I'm going to rip out her liver!" Sally's demon said. "And chew it down with a bottle of beer." She took another step closer. "Give me your liver!"

"Wait!" Cindy cried. "You can't eat my liver. It will make you sick. I had hepatitis as a little girl."

The three demons stopped in their tracks.

"Where did you get hepatitis?" Adam's demon asked quietly.

"In Mexico," Cindy said honestly. "When I was five years old my father took us to Cancun on vacation. You're not supposed to drink the local water, but I did anyway and I got real sick. When I returned to the States, my mother took me to a doctor who said I had hepatitis. I was sick for several weeks, and as yellow as a banana."

Adam's demon frowned. "What kind of hepatitis did you catch? Was it type A? Type B? Type C?"

"I don't know," Cindy said. "It was one of those."

"What difference does it make?" Sally's demon asked. "Let's eat the rest of her and leave her liver alone."

"It makes a big difference," Watch's demon said. "If she caught type B or C she could still be a carrier of the virus. If we eat her, any part of her, we might get sick."

Sally's demon snorted. "That's ridiculous!"

"It also happens to be accurate," Adam's demon said.

Cindy smiled in relief. "Yeah, you don't want to get sick. Now that I think about it, I had type B. Yeah, I'm definitely a carrier of the virus. But that's

OK. There's plenty of food here. Just have one of these slabs of beef. Really, I don't mind cooking you something to go with it. I'm a great cook. My mother always works long hours and I have to do most of the cooking. I'm flexible, too, when it comes to requests. Anyway you want your food is fine with me. You can have it spicy or bland." She added quietly, "Just don't eat me."

The demons looked at one another. "She could be lying about the hepatitis," Sally's demon said.

"If we did a blood test we'd know for sure," Watch's demon said.

"We can't do a blood test," Adam's demon snapped. "We're in a freezer, not a medical laboratory. Besides we're demons. We don't know how to do blood tests." The demon suddenly stopped and glanced over his shoulder. "Wait a second. We *are* in a freezer."

Watch's demon put a hand out to steady himself. "And the door's locked. That's bad. The cold's bad."

Sally's demon swayed and pointed a claw at Cindy. "She tricked us to come in here! It's her fault! Let's kill her!"

The three demons nodded in agreement and turned on her.

"No!" Cindy cried, backing into a wall. "If you eat me you'll get sick! Remember?"

"We can kill you without eating you," Adam's demon said, now only three feet away. Ignoring her burning flare, he reached out with his gross scaly hand and grabbed her by the hair. Yet he seemed to be moving in slow motion, and Cindy realized the cold was finally getting to him and the others. If she could just delay one minute more, she'd probably be all right. Adam's demon added, "Do you have any final words?"

"Yes," Cindy said quickly, stalling for time. "Just before you kill me I want to say that it's been a pleasure meeting demons like you. I understand you come from a poor neighborhood and that I can't judge you by my standards—when I have had every advantage in life. It would be completely unfair. Really, considering where you guys started, you've come pretty far. I just wanted to congratulate you."

Watch's demon seemed impressed, although he continued to sway as he spoke, almost as if he could no longer feel his legs. "That is awfully gracious of you. You're one of the few humans we've met who understands how difficult it is to grow up a demon."

"Yes, it's a hard life," Adam's demon said, yawning heavily. "But we try not to complain. Our motto is, If it hurts, it can always hurt more."

Sally's demon staggered and bumped into a side of beef, setting the red meat swaying back and forth in the gruesome red light of the flare. "Enough compliments," she said. "Open her throat and let her bleed to death. We have to find a way out of here."

Adam's demon nodded and moved a claw up to her throat. He tried to grip her neck, but his fingers were having trouble working.

"I'm sorry I have to do this, but we are the bad guys," he said. "We're supposed to do bad things. It's our nature."

Cindy met his gaze and suddenly she didn't feel afraid, even though she had begun to shiver violently from the cold. "You can't hurt me," she said simply.

"We're not going to hurt you," Watch's demon said, now hanging on to the wall for support. "We're going to kill you. That's an important difference."

"Yeah, when you're dead, you rot," Sally's demon gasped, staggering about.

"I'm not dying," Cindy said. "Not today at least." And with that she reached up and gave

Adam's demon a sharp shove, and the monster toppled backward and fell.

He didn't get up. He couldn't.

Watch's and Sally's demons stared in amazement.

"Hey, guys," Adam's demon called from the floor. "Give me a hand. This icy floor is sticking to my head."

"Give yourself a hand," Watch's demon snapped as he fell and landed on one knee. "I'm too cold to help you."

"We have to get out of here," Sally's demon moaned. But those were her last words because right then she collapsed and lay unconscious. Cindy could see the other two were slipping under the spell of the cold. Taking a large step over Adam's demon—who didn't even try to grab her—she stepped to the freezer door and pounded on it.

"Bryce!" she shouted. "You can open the door now!"

A few seconds later Bryce cracked the door a couple of inches and peered inside. Seeing her alive and well, he broke into a wide grin.

"Are they out cold?" he asked.

She glanced over her shoulder. Watch was now lying facedown, and the three of them had stopped moving completely. "Yeah," she said. "They're down for the count."

Bryce opened the door all the way. "How did you stop them from eating you?"

"I have a bad liver."

"What?"

Cindy smiled and patted him on the back. "It's a long story. Come on, we better get these monsters up to the cemetery and get the portal open for our friends." She paused. "And they are *your* friends, too. It's still your plan that's going to save them."

Bryce shook his head as he stared at the frozen demons. "You get all the credit, Cindy. What you just did was the bravest act I ever saw in my life. I'll have to tell Sally about it."

"She'll never believe you," Cindy said.

# 14

**W**atch was not doing well. Incredibly, Bloodbutton seemed to have detailed knowledge of everything Watch had ever done wrong. Every time the demon brought up another incident, Watch barely bothered to defend himself. Another gold coin would be put on the opposite side of the scale.

Most of these "sins" were small. Watch had stolen a cookie from a cookie jar when he was five. Watch tracked mud on the carpet when he was eight. But the way Bloodbutton told about the incidents, one would have thought Watch had murdered children in their sleep.

Foulstew would prompt Watch to remember his noble deeds, but Foulstew seemed to have no record of this good stuff Watch had done. Or if he did he kept it to himself. Watch had to supply that information himself.

Finally they got up to the point in his life when Adam moved to Spooksville and met Watch. By then Watch was about twenty gold coins in the hole.

"Now isn't it true," Bloodbutton said as he paced in front of Watch, "that you talked your friend, Adam—on the very day you met him—into accompanying you on a dangerous journey on the Secret Path?"

Watch shrugged. "I thought he wanted to go."

"You *thought?*" Bloodbutton snapped. "You risked a young man's life just because you *thought* he wanted to go on such a foolish journey? Did you explain to him that there was an excellent chance he could die on this journey?"

"Bum told us all it was dangerous," Watch said.

"Bum told him!" Bloodbutton exclaimed. "What about you? We're talking about you here. You're the one who risked your friend's life."

Watch shook his head. "I don't remember."

Bloodbutton grinned and gestured to the judge. "Another three gold coins against the accused!"

The judge pounded with his skull. "Scalekeeper, add three gold coins against Watch."

Foulstew stepped forward. He glanced anxiously at the jury and then at Watch. "Did you do anything noble on this first journey through the Secret Path."

Watch considered. "I can't remember."

"Watch," Adam called. "You saved my life by jumping on the back of the Black Knight in the cemetery."

"Objection!" Bloodbutton shouted. "That noble deed must be struck from the books! The defendant did not remember it himself."

The judge pounded his skull. "Sustained."

Watch frowned. "I saved Sally's life as well by jumping on the Black Knight's back."

"Did you risk your life to do so?" Foulstew asked.

"I guess," Watch said. "The Black Knight almost killed me."

"Objection!" Bloodbutton cried. "Same noble deed."

Foulstew addressed the judge. "It isn't exactly the same deed, not technically. He was saving another person. Also, he remembered by himself that he saved Sally. No one had to tell him." He glanced at the angry jury and added quietly, "I think he should get some credit for it."

The judge considered. Then he picked up his big black book and leafed through it. The judge muttered to himself as he slobbered on the pages.

"Let's see here, what is the boon when one human risks his life to save another human? We haven't had one of these in a long time. Ah, yes, here it is." The judge's face fell. "Oh no."

"What is it?" Bloodbutton asked, worried.

The judge looked miserable. "By the rules, the defendant must be granted a credit of ten gold coins for risking his life to save another human being."

"Ten?" Bloodbutton protested. "That's absurd. A human's life is hardly worth a single gold coin."

The judge glared at the prosecutor. "Are you questioning my interpretation of the law? This is what the book says." He spoke to the Scalekeeper. "Remove ten coins from the balance."

Adam whispered to Foulstew, who stood nearby. "Who wrote that book of rules?" he asked.

Foulstew shook his head. "It sure wasn't a demon."

"If he gets so much credit for saving a life," Sally said to Foulstew. "Tell him to list all the times he saved our lives."

"I don't want to do that," Foulstew said.

"Is it against the rules?" Adam asked.

"No," Foulstew said. "I'm allowed to advise him. But if you guys all get away, the jury might eat me for dinner."

"Come on," Sally said. "This is a chance to win the case of your life. Even if they eat you, you'll be remembered as the greatest demon lawyer the Dark Corner ever saw. Think about that. They'll toast your exploits with blood in every demon bar in town."

The idea seemed to appeal to Foulstew. He stepped forward, puffed on his cigar, and flicked the ash in the direction of the jury. Then he addressed Watch.

"Young man," he said, "jumping on the Black Knight's back was a brave act. Have you ever performed any other such brave acts?"

"You mean, have I ever saved my friends before?" Watch asked.

"Careful what you say," the judge said to Foulstew. But Foulstew didn't seem to hear him.

"Exactly," Foulstew said, glancing at Bloodbutton and smiling. "Tell us about every time you risked your life for your friends.'"

"Objection!" Bloodbutton shouted.

"Shut up!" the judge shouted back, leaning his bulk forward as if to hear better. "It's too late for that. The defendant may speak."

That was the end of that. Watch was able to list not less than a dozen times he saved his friends: with the aliens; the Cold People; the witch; the Howling Ghost; in the Haunted Cave. The list went on and on. The Scalekeeper was forced to keep removing the gold coins, and no matter how quickly Bloodbutton tried to add a few more small misdeeds, the scale kept tilting in Watch's favor. Soon he was sitting all the way down on his side and Bloodbutton had thrown up his arms in despair.

"Bring up the next defendant!" Bloodbutton said.

The judge simmered, mainly in Foulstew's direction. "You are free to go, Watch. But please remain in the court until your friends have been judged."

"Thank you, Your Honor," Watch said, climbing off the scale and flashing a rare smile.

"Adam Freeman will now sit on the scale!" the judge shouted, pounding his table with his skull.

Going through Adam's life while he still lived in

Kansas City, Bloodbutton was able to make a significant case against Adam. Of course Adam had never saved anyone's life in his old hometown because none of his friends had done things from which they needed to be saved. But once they got up to the time of Adam's moving to Spooksville, Adam was able to name ten times that he had saved his pals from death. He got so much credit so fast the judge was forced to let him go. Smiling, Adam returned to his friends. He spoke to Sally.

"Just mention all the times you rescued us," Adam said. "We'll be out of here in no time."

But Sally was nervous. "But I wasn't the hero as many times as you were."

"Now she tells us," Watch said.

"Sara Wilcox to the scale!" the judge ordered.

Sally started out all right, better than the others in fact. It seemed as a small kid she had seldom misbehaved. But when they passed her tenth birthday, Sally began to lose points dramatically. It seemed that bad-mouthing another person counted for one gold coin each, and Sally had done little else for the last two years.

"Isn't it true you insulted Cindy the day you met her?" Bloodbutton demanded.

Sally stood uneasily. "She deserved the insults.

She was trying to hit on Adam and she had just met him."

"Two gold tokens against the defendant!" Bloodbutton shouted to the judge. "She not only committed the crime, she has no remorse about it!"

The judge pounded his skull. "Make it three tokens, Scalekeeper!"

Naturally, Sally gained ground when her heroic deeds were listed. Saving Cindy in the Haunted Cave from a goblin spear counted for a lot because Sally had almost taken the spear in the side. Yet as the trial began to wind down, Sally was still five tokens down and bobbing up toward the ceiling. Bloodbutton spoke about the incident with the Howling Ghost.

"So you stayed down below while your friends Adam and Cindy went up to fight with the Howling Ghost?" Bloodbutton asked.

"That's true," Sally admitted. "But when Adam was thrown through the wall and over the railing of the lighthouse, I was there to save him. In fact, I risked my own life when I reached out to grab him. I could have been pulled over the edge and killed."

The judge nodded reluctantly to the Scalekeeper. "Remove ten tokens from the scale."

"Just a moment, Your Honor!" Bloodbutton

cried. "We are not through with the Howling Ghost incident. Isn't it true, Sara Wilcox, that when everything was over that night and everybody was safe you took credit for ideas that Watch provided to help Adam and Cindy defeat the Howling Ghost?"

"How do you know that?" Sally asked.

"It doesn't matter," Bloodbutton said. "Did you?"

Sally stammered. "I don't understand the question?"

"Demon prosecutors don't repeat questions!" Bloodbutton yelled. "Answer yes or no! Remember, you are under oath. If you lie, we will press your face into a vat of boiling lava this instant."

Sally paused and looked over at Watch. "Yes, I took credit for Watch's idea. He was the one who figured out the Howling Ghost was actually related to Cindy."

The judge pounded his skull. "Scalekeeper! Leave those ten gold tokens alone. A liar cannot be counted a hero." He paused and surveyed the courtroom, picking at his nose in the process. "Sara Wilcox, we have completed your life review and you are found wanting. Have you anything else to say in your miserable defense?"

Sally looked as if she were about to cry. But suddenly her old toughness surfaced. She straightened herself up and spoke to the entire assembly.

"I have been accused of bad-mouthing my friends and enemies," she said. "To these accusations I have no defense. So I did mouth off from time to time. So what? I'm young. I have a right to complain. But I will say, before being sentenced, that you demons are the sorriest-looking bunch of monsters I have ever seen. You live in a dump and you smell like garbage." She raised her voice. "I take it as a compliment to be found guilty by a bunch of losers like you!"

Naturally, her remarks did not go over very well. Bloodbutton requested ten eternal lives of agony for Sara Wilcox and the judge nodded his head vigorously. All the while the jury leaned forward, panting as if they couldn't wait to get their teeth on Sally. Watch kept shaking his head and Foulstew looked both relieved and disgusted at the same time. Altogether, the situation seemed pretty hopeless. It was then that Adam shouted over the din.

"You cannot take our friend!" he yelled.

His words quieted the courtroom, but the judge was smiling contemptuously. "Your friend will be found guilty, Adam," he said. "Have no doubt about that. You may as well say your goodbyes now."

The realization finally hit Sally that she was doomed. "Goodbye, guys. Sorry I wasn't the super heroes you were. I promise I won't ever criticize you again."

"Soon you won't have a tongue to criticize anyone with." Bloodbutton snickered.

"Don't gloat over your victory," Foulstew told him. "It's disgraceful."

"You cannot take our friend!" Adam repeated loudly. "We won't let you!"

The judge chuckled and closed his black book. "You have no choice in the matter. Just be thankful you and Watch have managed to escape our judgment. You won't be so lucky next time."

"We don't want to escape," Adam said. "We'll make you a counteroffer. If you release Sally, both of us will stay here in her place."

Watch cleared his throat. "Adam. Hmm, don't you want to discuss this?"

Adam ignored him. "You will have two of us for her," he said to the judge. "All we ask is that you return Sally to our world."

"Adam," Watch said.

Foulstew suddenly clapped his hands together. He went to shout out something but the judge silenced him with a sharp look. Once more the judge leaned over his wide table and stared down at Adam and Watch.

"Do you honestly mean to make this offer?" he asked.

"Yes," Adam said without hesitation. He bumped Watch and whispered under his breath. "Say yes."

"Well," Watch said.

Foulstew hissed under his breath. "Say yes!"

"Objection!" Bloodbutton shouted.

"Yes or no, Watch?" the judge asked.

Watch glanced around the courtroom, at the hungry jury, the evil prosecutor, the troubled judge. Finally his eyes came to rest on Sally. She continued to stand with her head bowed, looking more frail than he had ever seen her. Watch came to a decision.

"Yes, Your Honor," he said. "With my friend, Adam, I offer my life to save hers."

Sorehead jumped with excitement. "Good show, man!"

At that the courtroom went insane. Foulstew ran over to Watch and Adam and embraced them.

"There is a rule in our book," he said excitedly. "If two or more people offer to give their lives in our court to save the life of another, then all must go free. The rule has never been used before today, but neither the judge nor the jury has the power to overrule it." Foulstew turned to the judge. "Isn't that true?"

The judge was studying the fine print in his big black book. "That's true, I hate to say. Not only that. Those who have offered their lives to save Sara Wilcox are also permitted to ask a favor of the court."

"Objection!" Bloodbutton howled.

"Overruled!" the judge said.

"What kind of favor?" Adam asked.

The judge hesitated. "A legal favor. It is up to you to choose it."

Adam glanced at Watch and smiled. "Are you thinking what I'm thinking?"

Watch nodded. "I hate to leave any prisoners behind."

Adam addressed the court. "Our request is simple, but we want it carried out immediately. We want all the prisoners in the Dark Corner released. We want an end to all suffering in this dimension."

Of course this request raised a stink.

But the court had no choice. Even the demon court.

They had to obey the rules in the book.

# Epilogue

**F**oulstew escorted Adam, Sally, and Watch to the interdimensional portal. As if on cue, Bryce and Cindy stuffed three frozen demons through the tombstone, opening the magic doorway so that they could get back to where they belonged. It was then and only then that Watch and Adam finally trusted Bryce. They could hear him and Cindy yelling on the other side to hurry and return. But Foulstew seemed sad to see them go. He handed Adam his business card.

"If you have any legal problems in the future, be sure to give me a call," he said.

"We will," Adam promised, studying the card and then putting it in his back pocket. He was surprised to see that the demon had a fax machine.

"Have you ever met your human counterpart?" Watch asked, curious.

"No, but I've heard a lot about him," Foulstew said. "He's supposed to have visited here several times. I heard he's mayor of your town, or at least he used to be mayor."

Sally laughed. "Bum! I should have known. You two have a lot in common!"

"Tell me," Adam said to Foulstew. "That book of rules you have—it really helped us out. Do you know who wrote it?"

But Foulstew just winked as he turned and walked away.

"You'll have to ask Bum that question. He's the only one who knows."

"Ask that worthless old tramp?" Sally muttered as they got ready to return home. "Why does he have so much secret knowledge?"

"Careful what you say about him," Adam said.

Sally stopped and then burst out laughing. "Yeah, I forgot already! Someone somewhere is keeping score!"

## About the Author

Little is known about Christopher Pike, although he is supposed to be a strange man. It is rumored that he was born in New York but grew up in Los Angeles. He has been seen in Santa Barbara lately, so he probably lives there now. But no one really knows what he looks like, or how old he is. It is possible that he is not a real person, but an eccentric creature visiting from another world. When he is not writing, he sits and stares at the walls of his huge haunted house. A short, ugly troll wanders around him in the dark and whispers scary stories in his ear.

Christopher Pike is one of this planet's best-selling authors of young adult fiction.